Nettie's

MW00938980

Story by Roz Rosenbluth
Illustrations by Kristine Dillard

"I can't eat this piece of spaghetti," said Nettie. "It's too long."

"How long can a piece of spaghetti be?" asked her mother.

"It's so long I can walk the dog with it."

"Jump rope with it."

4

"I can fly a kite with it."

"It's so long I can use it
as a high wire."

"Rope a calf with it
or knit a sweater."

"It's so long I can tie up
a crook with it."

"I can swing from a bell
or tie it to a rocket."

9

"It's so long..." said Nettie.
Nettie's mother said,
"I'm sorry I asked."

Your spaghetti story was so long
that my soup got cold.
It was so long that the chicken burned.
It was so long..."

Nettie said, "I think I'll cut it up."
"Good idea," said Nettie's mother.